The Sleepy Book

A Lullaby

JUDY HINDLEY

The Sleepy Book

A Lullaby

illustrated by PATRICE AGGS

ORCHARD BOOKS
New York

Orchard Books
387 Park Avenue South
New York, NY 10016
Manufactured in the United States of America
Printed by General Offset Company, Inc.
Bound by Horowitz/Rae
Book design by Susan Phillips
The text of this book is set in 17 point New Caledonia.
10   9   8   7   6   5   4   3   2   1
Library of Congress Cataloging-in-Publication Data
Hindley, Judy.
The sleepy book : a lullaby / by Judy Hindley ; illustrated by Patrice Aggs. —
1st American ed.   p.   cm.
Summary: When the sun sets, some creatures retire to bed while others who
love the dark come out to celebrate the night.
ISBN 0-531-05971-5. — ISBN 0-531-08571-6 (lib. bdg.)
[1. Night — Fiction.   2. Sleep — Fiction.   3. Bedtime — Fiction.]
I. Aggs, Patrice, ill.   II. Title.
PZ7.H5696S1   1992   [E] — dc20   91-15787

To my dad and mother
for the first great stories
—J.H.

For John and Rachel
—P.A.

When the sun goes down
and the sky grows dim
and the shops are shut
and the buses stop…

When the cars go home
and the people go in...

mothers and fathers,
grandmas and grandpas,
uncles and aunts,
cousins and neighbors,
big kids and little kids
all go in…

(Well, almost all of them—
nearly all of them—
just about all of them
go in…)

When the shadows grow
and the night creeps round
and the lights go on
all over town...

Who loves the dark?

"We do," say the stars
at the top of the sky,
so far, so high.
"We love the dark."

"We do," say the owls
in a faraway tree.

There are the moon
and all of the stars.

Look out and find them
high in the air—

so tiny and few of them,
far and high,

brighter and brighter,
as night goes by,
thicker and brighter,
all over the sky—
hundreds and millions,
too many to count,

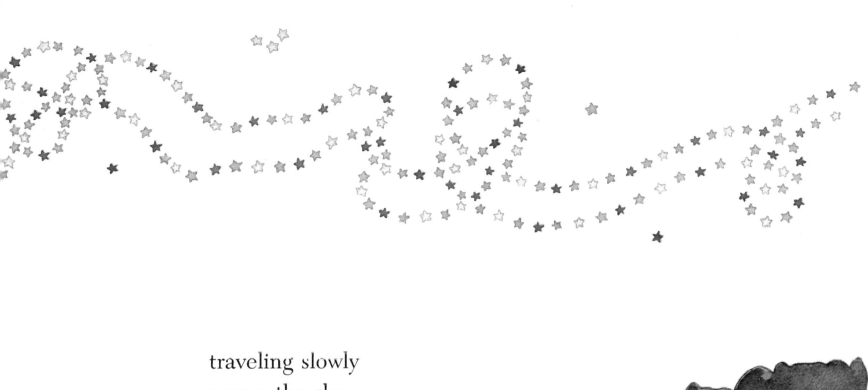

traveling slowly
across the sky—
steadily traveling
all night long—
and all through the night,
they're always there.

But the stars are far
and the stars don't speak.
Who else is there
who loves the dark?
Listen—
"Whoo
whoo
whoo—"

Can you hear an owl in a faraway tree?
Pretend you do,
though you know it's me.

Owls, freight trains,
foxes, mice,
all kinds of creatures
that burrow and creep
and come out to play
when we're asleep—

and last
all the streetlights
that march up and down
to take care of stragglers
coming home.

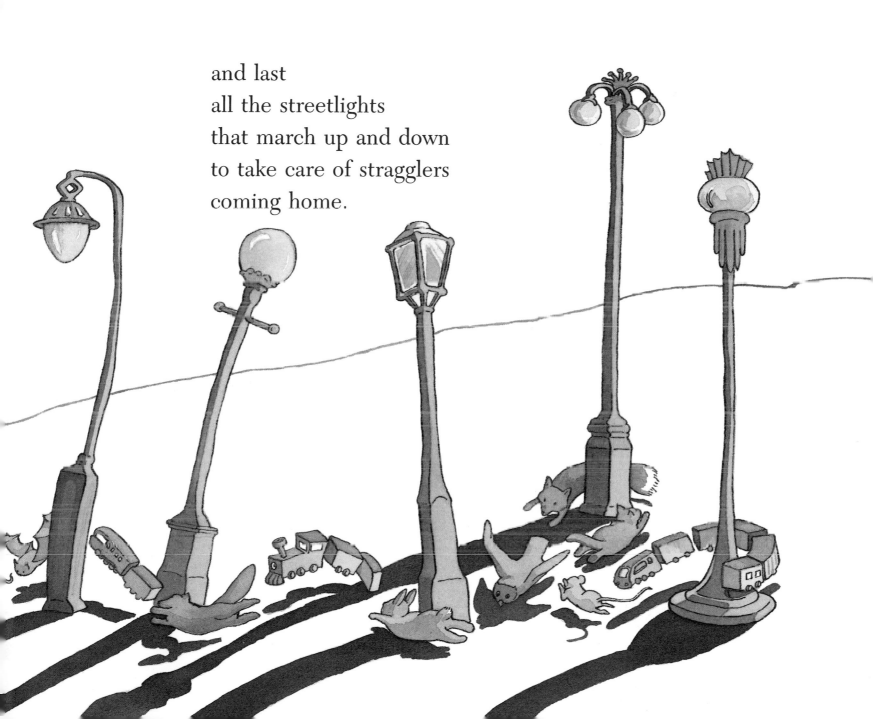

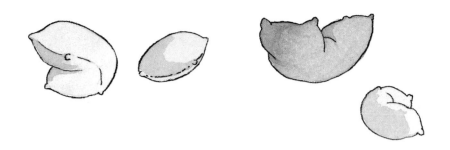

And look at us here,
so cozy and snug
wrapped up with a blanket,
wrapped up in a hug,
with a book and pillow,
and who else is there?

Is it your doll or your pig or your bear?
Is your bear getting sleepier now?
Are you?
I almost think
I'm sleepy, too....
And here we are,
so snug and tight.
Is it ever so peaceful
as when it's night?

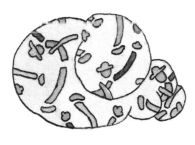

Are we ever so cozy
at any time
as the way we are
when it's dark outside?

Maybe you might almost say it's true
that we all love the dark.
I know I do.
How about you?

Lay down your head now.
Snuggle up tight.
Give me a kiss.
Turn off the light.

Sleep well, my dear.
Sweet dreams.

Good-night....